There Was an Old Man Who Painted the Sky

Teri Sloat

Pictures by **Stefano Vitale**

Christy Ottaviano Books

Henry Holt and Company ✦ New York

To the observant child in all of us —T. S.

To Slavik —S. V.

Henry Holt and Company, LLC, Publishers since 1866
175 Fifth Avenue, New York, New York 10010
www.HenryHoltKids.com

Henry Holt® is a registered trademark of Henry Holt and Company, LLC.

Distributed in Canada by H. B. Fenn and Company Ltd.

Library of Congress Cataloging-in-Publication Data
Sloat, Teri.
There was an old man who painted the sky / Teri Sloat ; illustrated by Stefano Vitale.—1st ed.
p.   cm.
Summary: In this song based on "The Old Woman Who Swallowed a Fly," a prehistoric man, contemplating the creation of the world,
paints images on the ceiling of a cave that are later discovered by a young Spanish girl in 1879.
ISBN-13: 978-0-8050-6751-4 / ISBN-10: 0-8050-6751-5
1. Children's songs, English—United States—Texts. 2. Altamira Cave (Spain)—Songs and music. [1. Altamira Cave (Spain)—Songs and music.
2. Cave paintings—Songs and music. 3. Art, Prehistoric—Songs and music. 4. Creation in art—Songs and music. 5. Songs.] I. Vitale, Stefano, ill. II. Title.
PZ8.3.S63245Tf 2009   782.42—dc22   [E]   2008018340

First Edition—2009 / Designed by Véronique Lefèvre Sweet
The artist used mixed media on board to create the illustrations for this book.
Printed in the United States of America on acid-free paper. ∞

1   3   5   7   9   10   8   6   4   2

Author's Note

The discovery of paintings on the ceiling of the Altamira Cave in 1879 changed the way the world viewed history. The young girl who discovered these paintings—Maria Marcelino—was not even nine years old. She was the daughter of jurist and amateur archaeologist Marcelino Sanz de Sautuola.

Don Marcelino had taken Maria with him to explore a cave on their property in northern Spain. It is said that while her father explored the floor of the cave looking for bones and stone tools, Maria looked up and saw the beautiful animal figures painted on the cave ceiling. Later research revealed that these paintings were between 11,000 and 19,000 years old. Those living during the time of the Stone Age used art to depict both the physical and spiritual worlds.

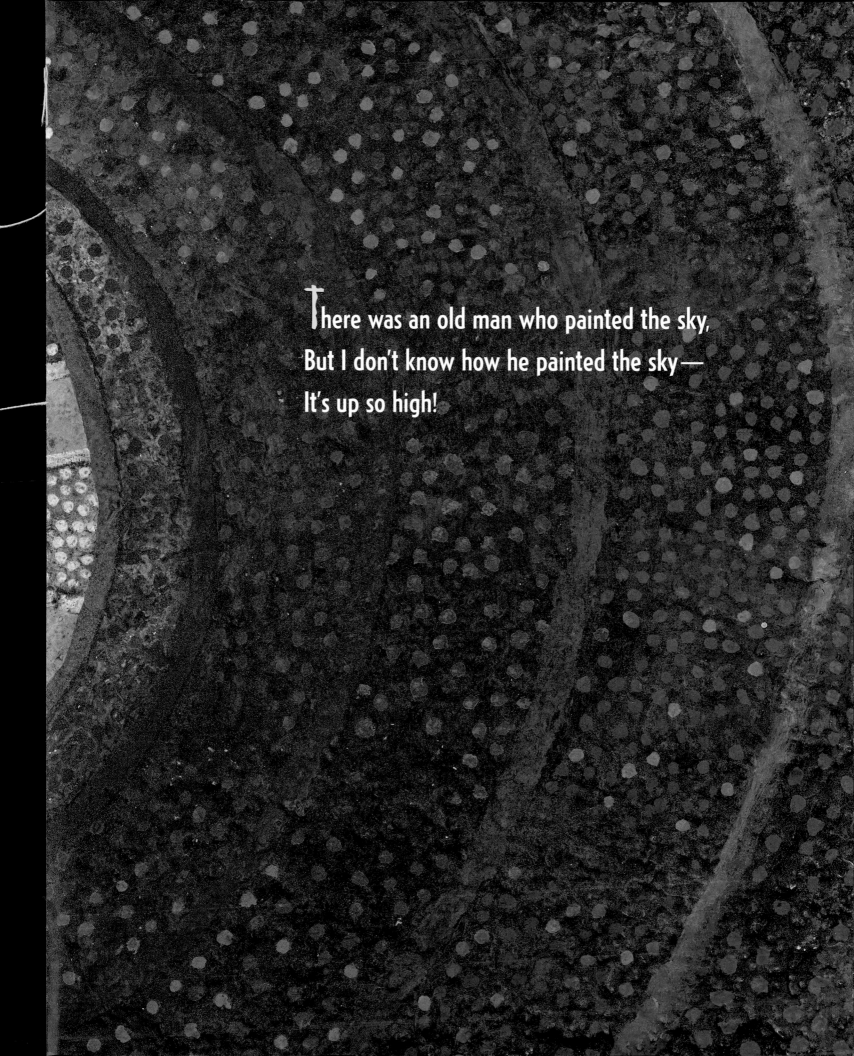

There was an old man who painted the sky,
But I don't know how he painted the sky—
It's up so high!

There was an old man who painted the night.
He splattered the stars and made the moon white.
He painted the night across the great sky,
But I don't know how he painted the sky—
It's up so high!

There was an old man who painted the sun
To shine next to night, and a day had begun.
He painted the sun to follow the night.
He painted the night across the great sky,
But I don't know how he painted the sky—
It's up so high!

There was an old man who flew round the sun,
Painting the planets that spun, one by one.
He painted the earth to circle the sun.
He painted the sun and a day had begun.
He painted the day to follow the night.
He painted the night across the great sky,
But I don't know how he painted the sky—
It's up so high!

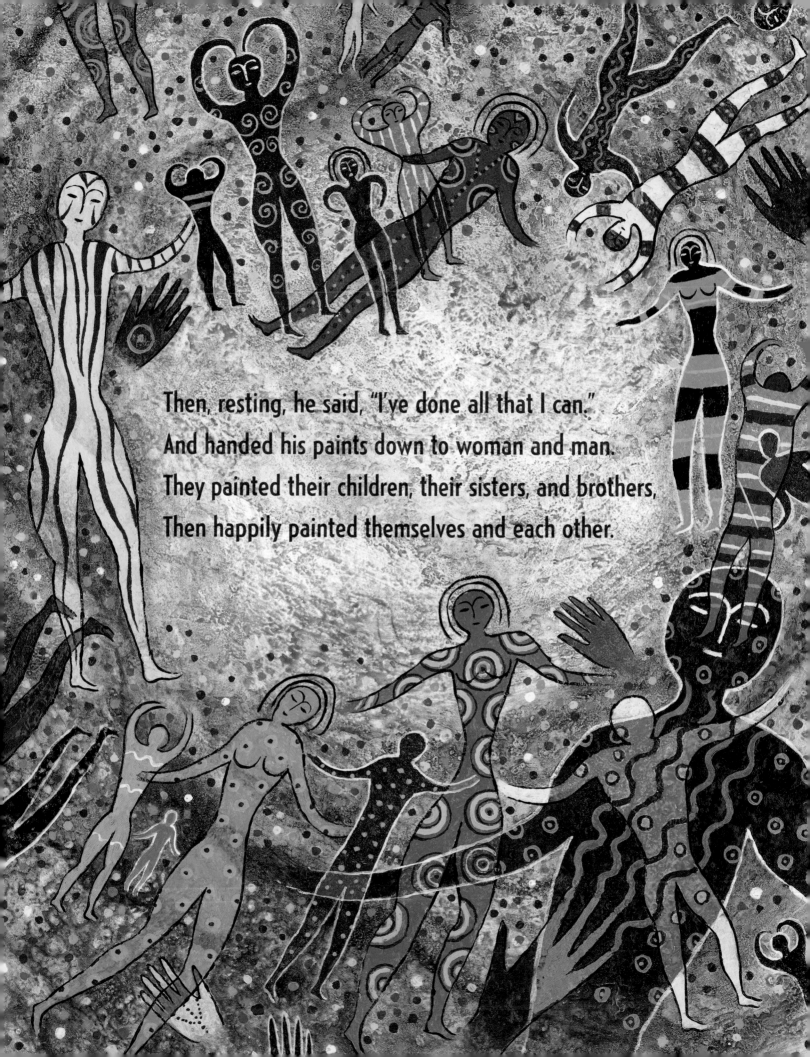

Then, resting, he said, "I've done all that I can."
And handed his paints down to woman and man.
They painted their children, their sisters, and brothers,
Then happily painted themselves and each other.

Beating their drums, they danced round the fire,
Spinning with joy, leaping higher and higher,
Till their colorful patterns, their spots, and their stripes
Flew off onto creatures that watched them that night.

There was earth with the planets that spun, one by one,
As they whirled through the sky, while they circled the sun.
She found the old man, painted high on the wall,
And she wondered and wondered as she looked at it all . . .

There was a young child in a cave all alone,
Who found the world round her painted on stone.
There were children like her; there was woman and man,
There were creatures of water and creatures of land.

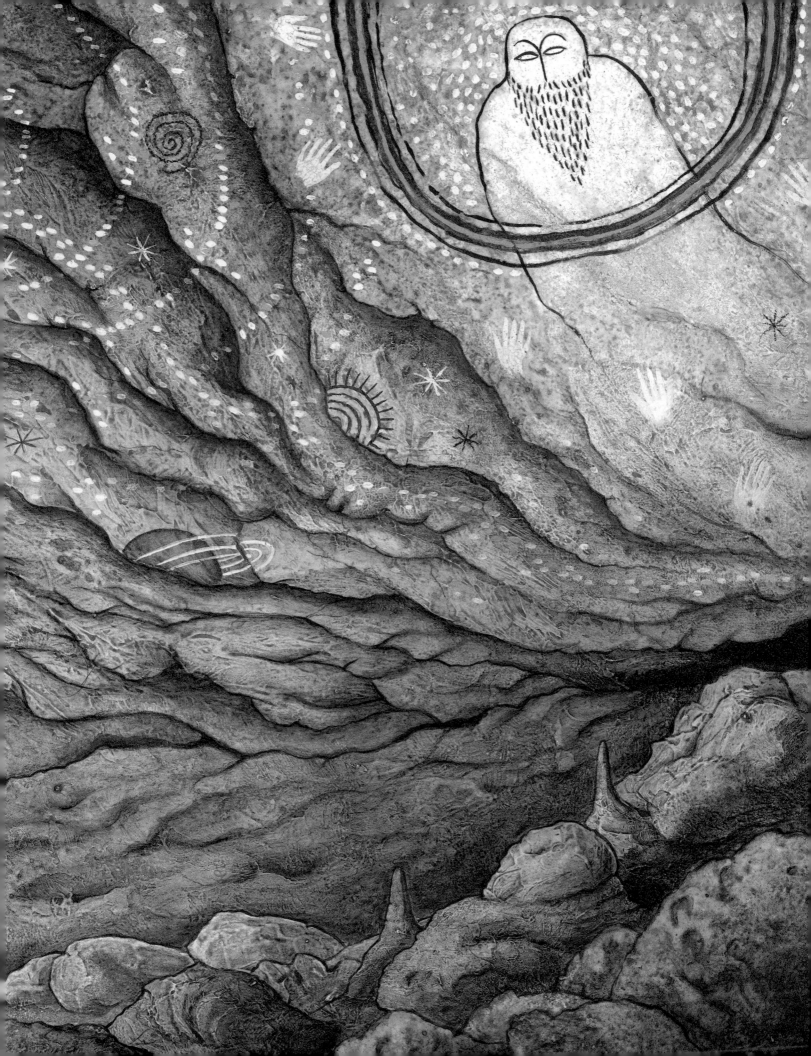

How did the old man paint the whole sky?
How did he do it?
It's up so high!